Travels of an
Extraordinary
Hamster

This edition first published in 2015 by Gecko Press
PO Box 9335, Marion Square, Wellington 6141, New Zealand
info@geckopress.com
English language edition © Gecko Press Ltd 2015
A catalogue record for this book is available from the
National Library of New Zealand

First American edition published in 2015 by Gecko Press USA,
an imprint of Gecko Press Ltd.
A catalog record for this book is available from the
US Library of Congress

Distributed in New Zealand by Upstart Distribution, www.upstartpress.co.nz
Distributed in Australia by Scholastic Australia, www.scholastic.com.au
Distributed in the UK by Bounce Sales & Marketing, www.bouncemarketing.co.uk
Distributed in the US by Lerner Publishing Group, www.lernerbooks.com

Original title: *Le voyage d'un hamster extraordinaire*
© 2014, Albin Michel Jeunesse

Written by Astrid Desbordes
Illustrated by Pauline Martin
Translated by Linda Burgess
Edited by Penelope Todd
Typesetting by Vida & Luke Kelly, New Zealand
Printed in China by Everbest Printing Co Ltd, an accredited ISO 14001
& FSC certified printer

ISBN paperback 978-1-927271-83-4

For more curiously good books, visit www.geckopress.com

Travels of an Extraordinary Hamster

GECKO PRESS

The snack

Simply hearing the voices of your loved ones — that's enough.

Or it's too much. I think I'll just take these with me.

Yes. They're so lucky. I'm going to visit them sometime. I want to get away from this boring clearing... From Hedgehog, Squirrel, Rabbit, Mo — umm, from everyone.

Good grief. Mole's already lost her sight, and now she's losing her mind. Oh dear.

Do-it-yourself

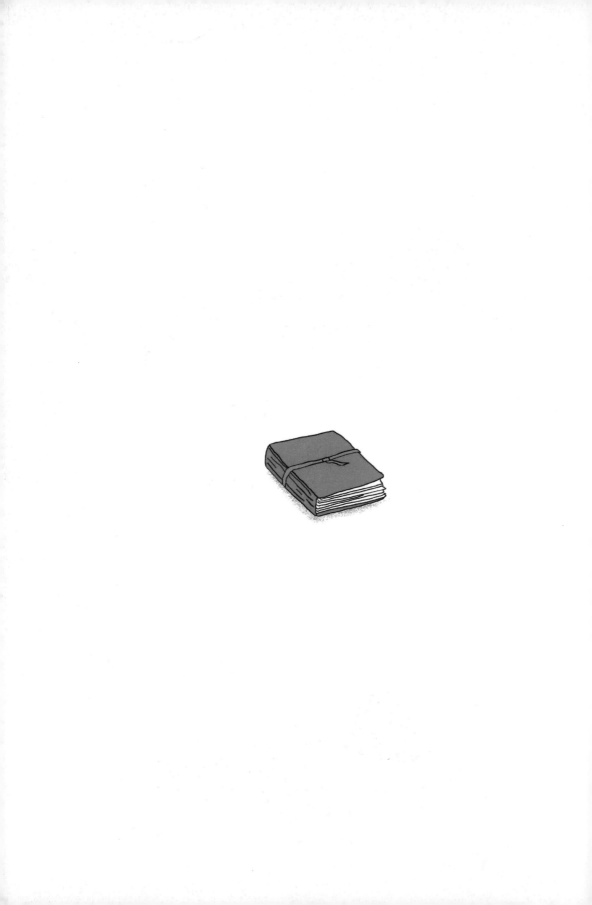

Writing
a letter

Invitation

Holidays

I'm leaving tomorrow
on a space mission.

I have been chosen unanimously
by Mole, Snail, Bear
and, of course, Rabbit
(who doesn't have a clue)...

...to speak to my lunar
cousins about Mole's
great work which is
dedicated to me.

This little break will do me a lot of good. However, the trip itself could be tiring.

I must get my strength up.

Until tomorrow, Dear Diary.

The glasses

The spaceship

Dear Diary

I'm just back after several
days on the moon.

My cosmic cousins were
absolutely astounded to meet
a marvellous creature like me.
One who's also the hero of
a novel.

But I managed to
reassure them and show
them my charm.

I even agreed
to become their
cosmic idol.

Now on the moon my portrait
adorns their buildings and
monuments, and even their
dinner plates.

It's most agreeable.

The return

Writing a letter
(continued)

snowshoes ... yes, good idea ...

And a nice fluffy jacket will come in handy.

Wonderful! I have a feeling I'm going to love the North Pole.

The arrival

Introductions

The snow

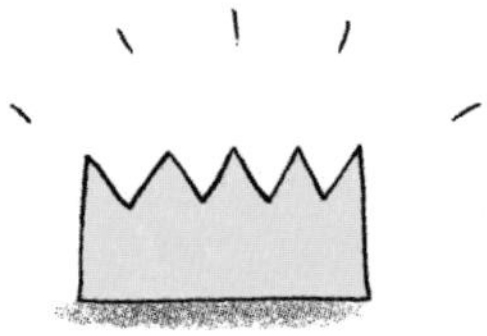

Distinguished titles

The palace

And what are these funny mounds of ice?

They're igloos. That's where you'll sleep.

Ha-ha, very funny, Penguin. I enjoy a good joke, but in the meantime I'd like to rest and have a meal.

In which case, follow me. You are my guests.

Regrettably, protocol doesn't allow Rabbit to dine with me. I'll come alone to the palace.

Goodbye, good Rabbit.

Dessert

91

Dear Diary

Yesterday, we arrived
on the ice.

It's been a delightful experience:
the seals and penguins are a little
rustic in their ways, but they have
a certain charm.

Ah! I do like
living simply.

But alas, I feel it's rather hard on Mole, Hedgehog, Rabbit, and the others.

Atchoo!

Pffftt!

And even though my presence reassures them, I think we'll be forced to go home tonight: Rabbit has taken ill.

The invitation

The ice skates

Dear Diary

HAMSTER

The ice-skating race has just finished. I'm tired but happy.

Winning was no easy matter. Of the 600 skaters who started, I alone crossed the finish line.

On the ice, emotions were high. Penguins in their thousands fainted as I passed by.

Even as I write, Mole
is still out there,
reviving spectators.

Ah, Dear Diary. From inside
my igloo, I hear the crowd
calling my name. How thrilling.

The countryside

Ice and ocean

Farewells

A letter for Mole

Dear Mole,

Even though you can't see a thing,
I love your way of looking at the world.
I love the way you speak,
the way you listen.
And I love the letters
that you never send me.

Signed: Hedgehog

Return to the clearing